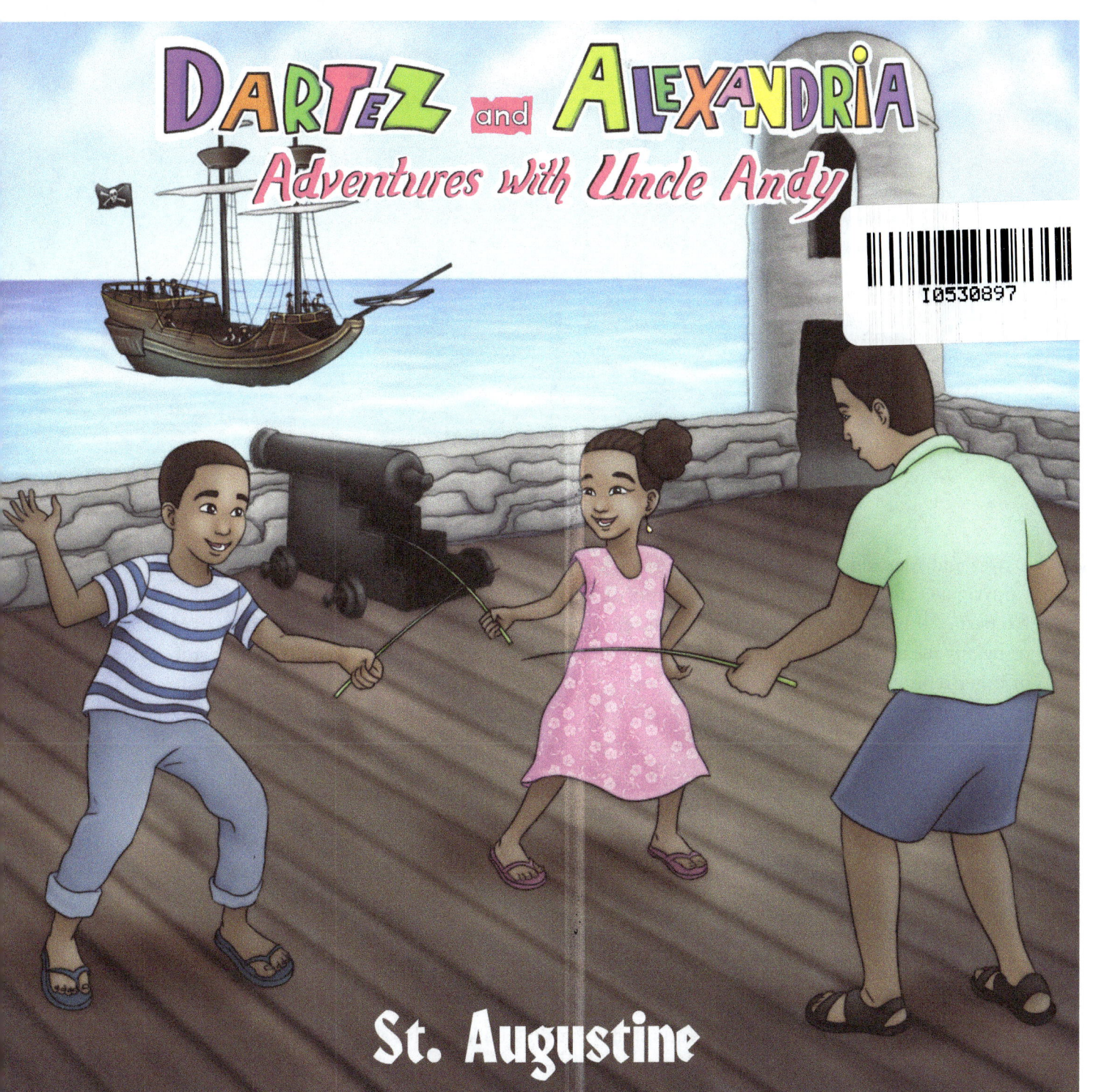

DARTEZ and ALEXANDRIA
Adventures with Uncle Andy

St. Augustine

Written by Anthony Eugene Brannon
Illustrated by Anthony Eugene Brannon and John Currie

I0530897

Dartez and Alexandria: Adventures with Uncle Andy, St. Augustine
Copyright© 2015 Anthony Eugene Brannon, all rights reserved
No part of this publication may be reproduced, stored in a retrieval system or transmitted, in any form or by any means, without the prior written permission of ATC Future, Inc. or, in case of photocopying or other reprographic copying, a license from ATC Future, Inc.

Published by ATC Future, Inc.
P.O. Box 26305, Jacksonville, Florida 32226
Printed in the United States of America

Copy Editor: Laurie B. Conaway
Book Designer: MALWEST design
First Edition   10 9 8 7 6 5 4 3 2 1

ISBN: 978-0-9863174-7-7

Contact ATC Future, Inc. at info@atcfuture.org regarding bulk purchases and other inquiries.

Also, visit the Dartez and Alexandria Book Club™ at www.DartezAndAlex.com

Spring had arrived early and Dartez and Alexandria were eager to go outside.

They hung up their coats and sweaters and pulled out their shorts and swimsuits. It was time for the official opening of the area beaches.

Uncle Andy had planned a beach get-a-way that to their surprise would include an American history lesson.

Just like his parents did when he was a kid, Uncle Andy loaded Dartez and Alexandria into the car along with beach towels and a water cooler.

They travelled to Saint Augustine Beach, Florida which was only an hour's drive from Dartez and Alexandria's home.

On their way to the beach, they stopped in the historic city of Saint Augustine.

One of the first things Dartez and Alexandria noticed was the Florida School for the Deaf and the Blind. Uncle Andy told them about the many times that he visited the school with his father who had two brothers to attend the school.

Uncle Andy's uncles learned how to read there and they also learned how to take care of themselves in the world outside of school.

The next thing to catch Dartez and Alexandria's eye was the entrance to the famous Fountain of Youth. Dartez immediately asked Uncle Andy if the fountain really kept people young. Uncle Andy laughed and said if that were so, you could buy it in a bottle.

The kids didn't waste much time there. Instead, they hurried to tour the Castillo de San Marco, a fort built to defend the Spanish settlement of Saint Augustine against challenges from the French.

The mighty fortress helped Saint Augustine become the oldest continuous settlement in the United States of America. It was established in the year 1565.

Before its discovery by the Spanish Admiral Pedro Menendez de Aviles of Puerto Rico, Saint Augustine was home to the Timucua who had built their own settlement in the area.

For more than 200 years, the Timucua, Spanish settlers and free blacks co-existed in a free society in Saint Augustine. Up until America's Civil War.

After the Civil War, business titans like railroad baron Henry Flagler began to develop coastal Florida along the route of his east coast railroad.

In Saint Augustine, Mr. Flager built the beautiful Ponce de Leon Hotel known today as the home of Flagler College.

Each year, millions of people from around the world travel to Saint Augustine to enjoy it's rich cultural heritage, early American buildings, and historic neighborhoods.

The historic neighborhood of Lincolnville was the setting of some important events during the Civil Rights Movement of the 1960's when African Americans and others fought for a more perfect America.

Uncle Andy explained to Dartez and Alexandria that it is because of the many brave people who lived in Saint Augustine throughout the centuries that we are all free to enjoy its rich history and beautiful beaches today.

"About those beaches," said Alexandria.
"Let's go and find one!"

"No problem kids", said Uncle Andy.
"I'll just park here on the sand."

www.ingramcontent.com/pod-product-compliance
Lightning Source LLC
Chambersburg PA
CBHW082251120626
46555CB00009B/3040